Luna and the BIG BLUR

A Story for Children Who Wear Glasses

by
Shirley Day

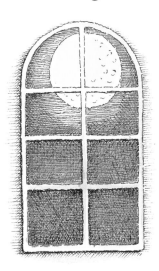

illustrated by
Don Morris

Magination Press • **New York**

To Jamie, my husband and best friend.
I love you bunches.

Library of Congress Cataloging-in-Publication Data
Day, Shirley
    Luna and the big blur : a story for children who wear glasses / by
Shirley Day ; illustrated by Don Morris.
        p.   cm.
    Summary: A young girl who hates her glasses learns to appreciate
them after spending a day without them.
    ISBN 0-945354-66-5.
    [1. Eyeglasses—Fiction.]   I. Morris, Don, ill.   II. Title.
PZ7.D3325Lu   1995
[E]—dc20
                                                                95-912
                                                                CIP
                                                                AC

Published by
Magination Press
An imprint of Brunner/Mazel, Inc.
19 Union Square West
New York, NY 10003

Manufactured in the United States of America

10 9 8 7 6 5 4 3 2 1

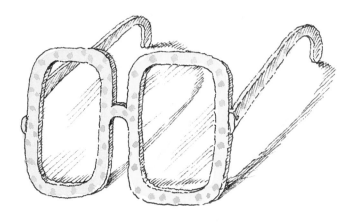

INTRODUCTION FOR PARENTS

Today many young children have to wear eyeglasses to see properly. The usage is so common that taunts of "four eyes" and other teasing are mostly a thing of the past.

Nonetheless, for every child, the realization that their eyesight is no longer perfect is a blow to self-esteem. Adjustment to wearing glasses can be a difficult task. Glasses may feel uncomfortable at first. They may also seem very inconvenient. For instance, where do you store them when you are not wearing them so you won't lose them or sit on them? Also, it may be hard to figure out how or when to use them for sports such as swimming or other activities.

Even when children are allowed to choose their own glasses, the wire or plastic, brightly colored or plain, frames can seem like a terrible intrusion on their faces. Children may have trouble recognizing themselves behind even the most fashionable look.

The story of *Luna and the Big Blur* acknowledges children's feelings of sadness and discomfort, while it reassures them that it is OK to wear glasses. They will laugh and have fun with Luna along the way of her adventures. And they will learn, as Luna does, that they have a lot to offer, with or without their glasses.

Luna thought she was named after a fish.

"Luna the Tuna." Why, oh why, didn't Mom and Dad name her Alex or Rachel or Sharon?

Luna liked her tiger cat named Plato. And she liked her bright colored shirts with squiggly lines and circles. And, she specially liked the arched window in her bedroom, through which she watched the moon in the night sky before she went to sleep.

But Luna didn't like her name. And she didn't like one other thing. Something she could not ignore. For whenever she crossed her eyes and looked down, there they were.

Her eyeglasses.

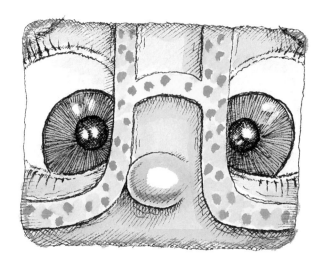

Sitting right on the middle of her nose, making small dents in her face.

Luna's mom had allowed Luna to choose the frame. She picked a yellow one with tiny red polka dots. But she still didn't like her glasses. When she looked in the mirror, they were all she could see.

She tried to make them less noticeable. She tried covering them up with her bangs, until Mom cut her hair.

She tried wearing her coat with the collar up, but she looked ridiculous.

She even tried walking around with her head tilted to the
ground. But of course that didn't last very long. "Ouch!"

Luna's mom owned a gift shop that sold the strangest and craziest things. "Simply wild!" customers would say. There was a clock that ran backwards and a string of lights that looked like

cream-filled cookies. In the corner was a plastic giraffe whose neck bent down when anyone made a loud sound.

Luna loved the store, and she loved her mom even more. But her mom did not need to wear glasses. Her eyesight was perfect.

Luna's dad taught science at the local high
school. He too had perfect vision and did not need to
wear glasses.

Luna's baby sister Kirstin was only a year old.
Luna could tell Kirstin her deepest secrets. "I hate
wearing glasses. Even with my favorite clothes, my
glasses stick out. It's not fair. Why me?"

One night, as Luna soundly slept, she dreamed that she was
on the moon, surrounded by huge sunflowers. An aqua pond was
filled with hundreds of little, jumping fish. She could see each one

clearly as it leaped out into the air. And the best part was—she wasn't wearing glasses. "I can see! No more glasses!"

When she woke up from her happy dream, Luna did not reach for her glasses. Instead she left her room cheerfully chanting, "I can see! No more glasses!"

"Look, Plato, no glasses," she said as she bent down to pet the cat. But as she came closer, Luna realized she was petting her mom's fuzzy slippers. "Oops."

Luna headed to the kitchen. Hmm, the soup smelled yummy. She grabbed a spoon and was about to dip it into the bowl when her mother exclaimed, "What are you doing? Get your spoon out of the fishbowl!"

  Luna had no trouble locating the ice cream in the freezer. After scooping some Peanut Butter Licorice Delight into a bowl, she decided to top it off with some fudge syrup. She grabbed the plastic bottle and began to squeeze. Thick gobs of ketchup squirted out. "Gross!" she yelled.

Luna still wanted to snack. "Oooh, munchies," she said as she grabbed an opened bag on the counter. "MMMEOOOWWW." Plato was suddenly on the counter, his nose pressed against Luna's. She was about to put the treats in her mouth when she realized she was holding cat biscuits. "Double gross!" she cried.

All day long, Luna tried hard to see. No matter how she squinted and stared, everything was still a big blur. She saw a blur on the sidewalk when she tripped over a pair of roller skates. The blurs in the living room turned into furniture when she bumped into them. Worst of all, the harder she tried to see, the more her head ached.

It finally dawned on her. Her happy dream wasn't true. She couldn't see without her glasses.

Luna headed to her room to put on her glasses and to get ready for bed. Along the way, she poked fun at herself. She sang, "Luna the Tuna, with glasses on her nose. Taking them everywhere, everywhere she goes."

Once in her room, she put on her yellow eyeglasses and let out a sigh. "Thank goodness. I can see again." She looked around the room and out her favorite window. Yes, she could see again, but she was still sad. She continued to sing, "Luna the Tuna, with glasses on her nose."

Her dad heard her go upstairs and came to say good night. "Luna, are you okay?" he asked.

"I don't know, dad. You see, I had this dream . . ." And Luna told him about her dream. She told him about the moon and the little fish and how happy she was she didn't need her glasses. "And Daddy, I know that I need my glasses. It's just . . . I'm the only one in our family who needs to wear them." At that moment, her eyes filled with tears.

"I know, Luna, but your eyes are different from ours. You were born nearsighted. You can see okay up close but not far away. The lenses on your glasses help you focus because the lenses in your eyes can't. Some people are farsighted and can see things at a distance but not up close. Mom and I see better than you now, but we might need glasses when we get older. And, maybe Kirstin will need a pair of glasses when she gets to be your age. Understand?" Luna nodded that she did.

"Besides glasses," said her dad, "there are other things that make you different."

"Like what?" Luna asked with a sniffle.

"Well, like your charming personality."

"Oh, Dad."

"And your wit. You're very clever and so curious about everything. Sometimes I wonder if I can answer your questions!

They're always such wonderful questions, like the one about wearing glasses.

"And," her dad continued, "you're named after something special. *You're* the only one in the family named after a certain object in the sky. One that's truly magical."

"Really?" Luna didn't understand.

"Yes, Luna is the name of the moon goddess."

"You named me after the moon?" Luna asked in delight.

"You better believe it, sweetheart. You see, one day before you were born, Mom and I were decorating your room. It was almost midnight when we got through. So we sat down to rest, and there, up in the sky, was a beautiful full moon shining through the window. We decided right then to name you Luna."

Luna was elated. "You mean you didn't name me after a fish?"

"Of course not. Where did you get such a silly idea? Now, do you feel better?" Luna nodded yes. "And now, back to this business about your glasses . . ."

"It's okay, Daddy, you won't have to worry about me. I don't mind wearing my glasses anymore." Luna gave her dad a hug and crawled under the blanket.

"Good night, Dad."

"Sweet dreams."

Luna removed her glasses from her face and wiped the lenses on the sleeve of her flannel pajamas.

Plato hopped on her bed and curled by her side. From her

bed, Luna stared at the big round moon in the sky, surrounded by tiny, flickering stars.

Glasses or not, her world never looked better.

MAGINATION PRESS BOOKS

Breathe Easy: Young People's Guide to Asthma
Cat's Got Your Tongue? A Story for Children Afraid to Speak
Clouds and Clocks: A Story for Children Who Soil
Double-Dip Feelings: Stories to Help Children Understand Emotions
Gentle Willow: A Story for Children About Dying
Gran-Gran's Best Trick: A Story for Children Who Have Lost Someone They Love
Homemade Books to Help Kids Cope: An Easy-to-Learn Technique for
    Parents and Professionals
I Want Your Moo: A Story for Children About Self-Esteem
Ignatius Finds Help: A Story About Psychotherapy for Children
Into the Great Forest: A Story for Children Away from Parents for the First Time
Jessica and the Wolf: A Story for Children Who Have Bad Dreams
Julia, Mungo, and the Earthquake: A Story for Young People About Epilepsy
Little Tree: A Story for Children with Serious Medical Problems
Luna and the Big Blur: A Story for Children Who Wear Glasses
Night Light: A Story for Children Afraid of the Dark
Otto Learns About His Medicine: A Story About Medication for Hyperactive Children
The Potty Chronicles: A Story to Help Children Adjust to Toilet Training
Proud of Our Feelings
Putting on the Brakes: Young People's Guide to Understanding
    Attention Deficit Hyperactivity Disorder (ADHD)
The "Putting on the Brakes" Activity Book for Young People with ADHD
Russell Is Extra Special: A Book About Autism for Children
Sammy the Elephant and Mr. Camel: A Story to Help Children Overcome Bedwetting
Sammy's Mommy Has Cancer
Sarah and Puffle: A Story About Diabetes for Children
Scary Night Visitors: A Story for Children with Bedtime Fears
Tanya and the Tobo Man: A Story in English and Spanish for Children
    Entering Therapy
This is Me and My Single Parent: A Workbook for Children and Single Parents
This is Me and My Two Families: A Workbook for Children in Stepfamilies
The Three Birds: A Story for Children About the Loss of a Loved One
What About Me? When Brothers and Sisters Are Sick
Wish Upon A Star: A Story for Children with a Parent Who Is Mentally Ill
You Can Call Me Willy: A Story for Children About AIDS
Zachary's New Home: A Story for Foster and Adopted Children